ordinary
terrible
things

ordinary
terrible
things

Dear Child,

Looks like you were born to make history.

The system of white supremacy shows itself in all its horror.

The people are showing ourselves, too—look how many!

Now, you, me, and everyone alive in this moment* get to be part of undoing what should never have been done.

We meet this moment with our hearts broken, many times over.

We meet it with the education we've gotten so far and a lot of listening and learning ahead of us.

We meet it breathing... and being still as we begin to understand.

We meet it with a burning, actually on-fire question: *What took so long?*

Now. Let's dismantle white supremacy everywhere—especially in our own minds and bodies.

This is the chance of a lifetime and you are free to embrace it.

With love and courage . . .

Anastasia
Brooklyn, New York
June 2020

*There is a note for you at the end of this book about *being alive in this moment*.

NOT MY IDEA

A BOOK ABOUT WHITENESS

Written and illustrated by
Anastasia Higginbotham

dottir
press

Published in 2018 by Dottir Press
33 Fifth Avenue
New York, NY 10003

Dottirpress.com

FIRST EDITION
Fifth printing: July 2020

Illustration and design by Anastasia Higginbotham
Photography by Alexa Hoyer
Production by Drew Stevens

Special thanks to Jennifer Baumgardner, Drew Stevens, Abraham Higginbotham,
Lisa Daniels, and Jon Luongo.
Pencil drawing on page 11 by Sabatino Luongo Higginbotham.
Additional editing by Lionel Luongo Higginbotham.

Library of Congress Cataloging-in-Publication Data is available for this title.
ISBN 978-1-9483-1000-7

Printed in the United States of America by Worzalla

In a 1993 interview, Toni Morrison said about racism in America: "White people have a very, very serious problem, and **they** should start thinking about what **they** can do about it." She added, "Take **me** out of it." Those words landed in me as a direct command.

I made this book for my own white sons with help from their teachers and mine. It's dedicated to the Brooklyn Free School, where my family was first called upon to engage with whiteness in order to dismantle white supremacy.

Deepest thanks to:

Ben Howort

Rev. angel Kyodo williams

Loretta Ross

Anyanwu Uwa

Randy Clancy

Noleca Anderson Radway

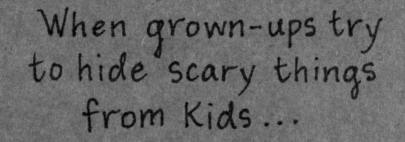

...it's usually
because they're
scared too.

Who is that with their hands up?
Why is that policeman screaming at him?

Our family is kind to everyone.

We don't see color.

Deep down we all know.

Color matters.

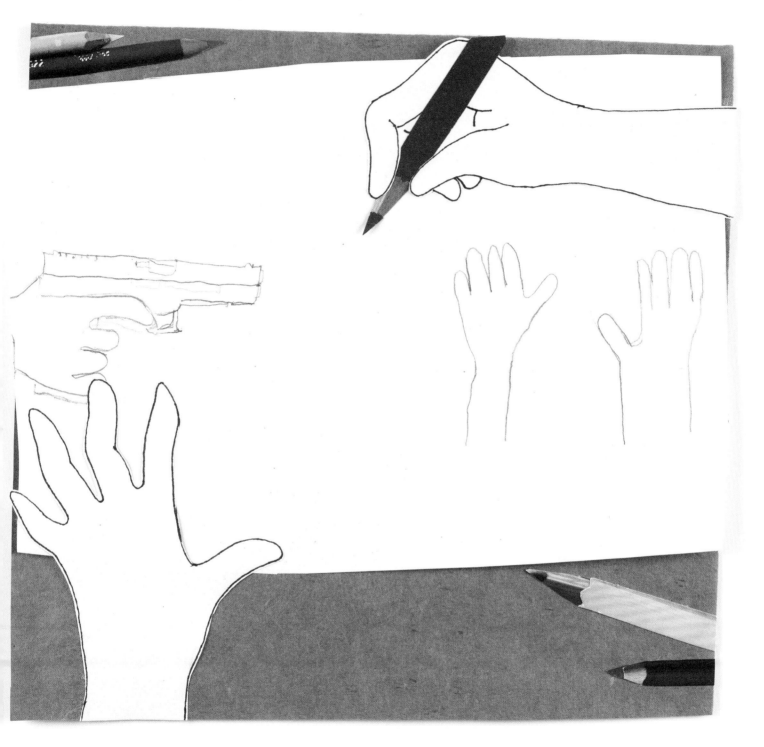

Skin color makes a difference
in how the world sees you
and in how you see the world.

It makes a difference in how

$15

SECURITY

14

much
trouble
seems
to
find you
or
let
you
be.

15

In stores,
in cars,
on sidewalks,
at school —

your skin color
affects the most
ordinary daily
experiences,

including...

... which neighborhoods welcome you.

19

You may get the message that racism is happening only to Black and brown people.

25

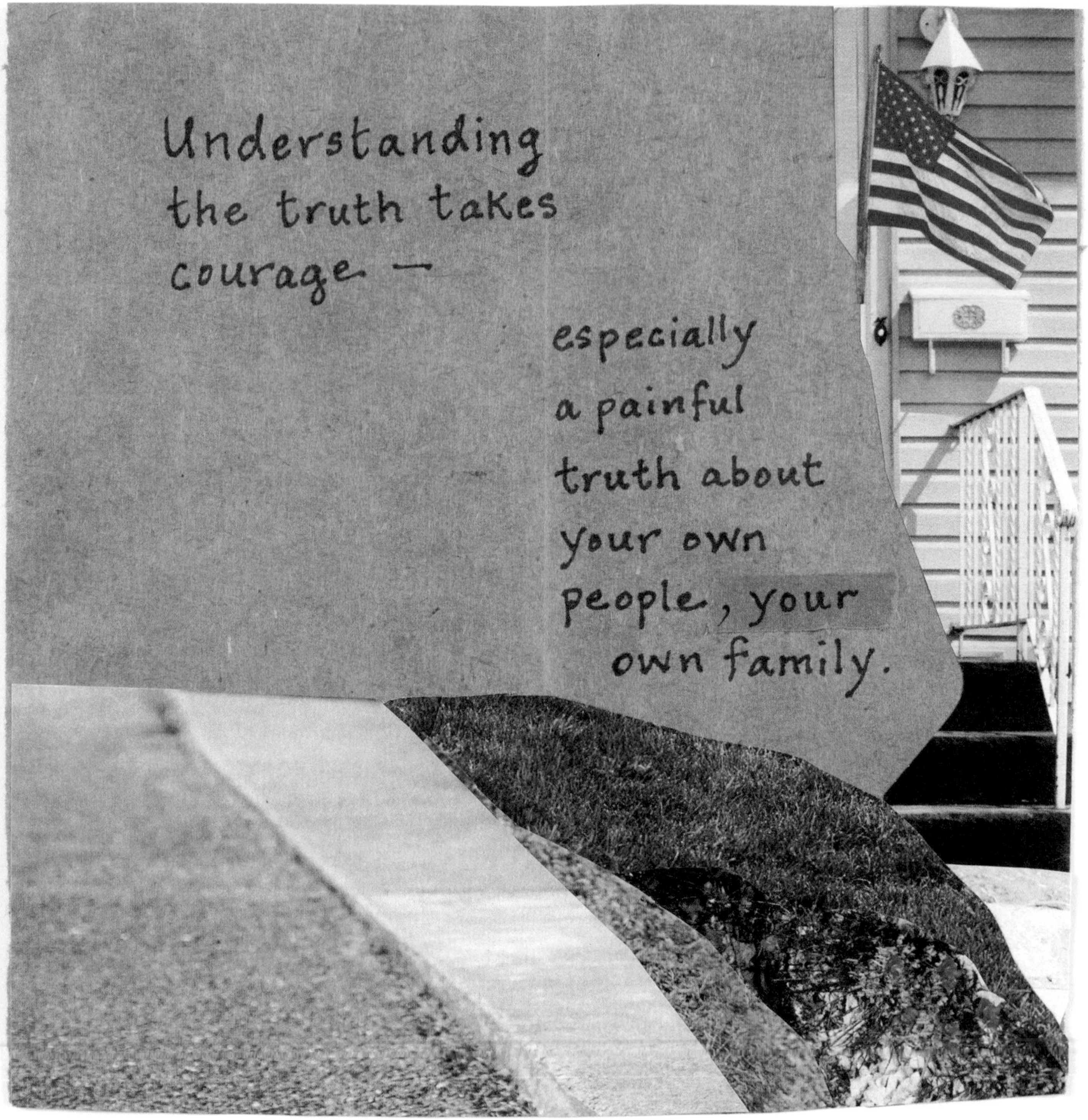

Understanding
the truth takes
courage —

especially
a painful
truth about
your own
people, your
own family.

27

Even people
you love
may behave
in ways
that show...

...they
think
they are
the
good ones.

29

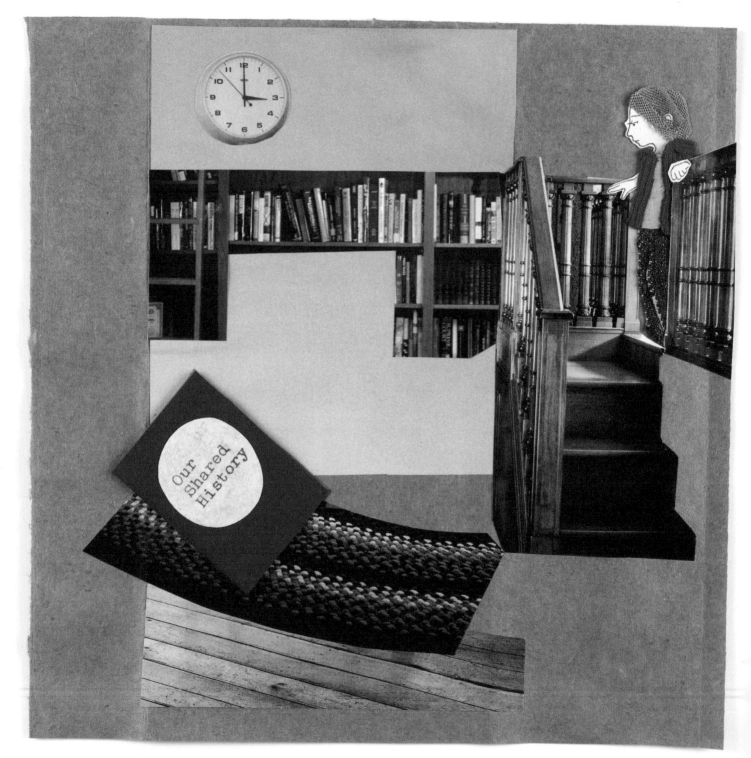

Our Shared History

In the United States of America, white people have committed outrageous crimes against Black people for four hundred years.

All along, every step of the way, people who love justice and love each other have been fighting back.

33

Many white people did things they **never** should have done.

Bank
Loan
$$$

DENIED

denied opportunity

NOTICE
OF
EVICTION

denied housing

Voter
Registration
TEST
Parts A,B,C
Pages 1-4
Sections 1-20

215 J

denied voting rights

Many other white people failed
to see the problem with this.

exploited the love and labor of Black women

Yes, ma'am.

These choices put wealth and power into white hands, homes, and neighborhoods.

Some white people joined the leaders of Black liberation.*

Angelina Grimké and Sarah Grimké, 1838

Abolitionists, Suffragists, Sisters

Julian Bond and members of the Student Nonviolent Coordinating Committee, 1963

*liberation = love + freedom

Nina Simone, 1967

Nuns and fellow marchers on the Selma to Montgomery March, 1965

Colin Kaepernick kneels, 2017

John Lewis and fellow demonstrators kneel, 1962

Racism is still happening. It keeps changing and keeps being the same.

And yet...
just being here,
alive in this moment,
you have a chance
to care about this,
to connect.

...like breaking.

45

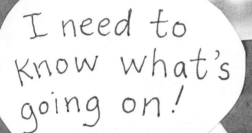

I do see color! I see yours, mine, and everybody's!
You can't hide what's right in front of me.

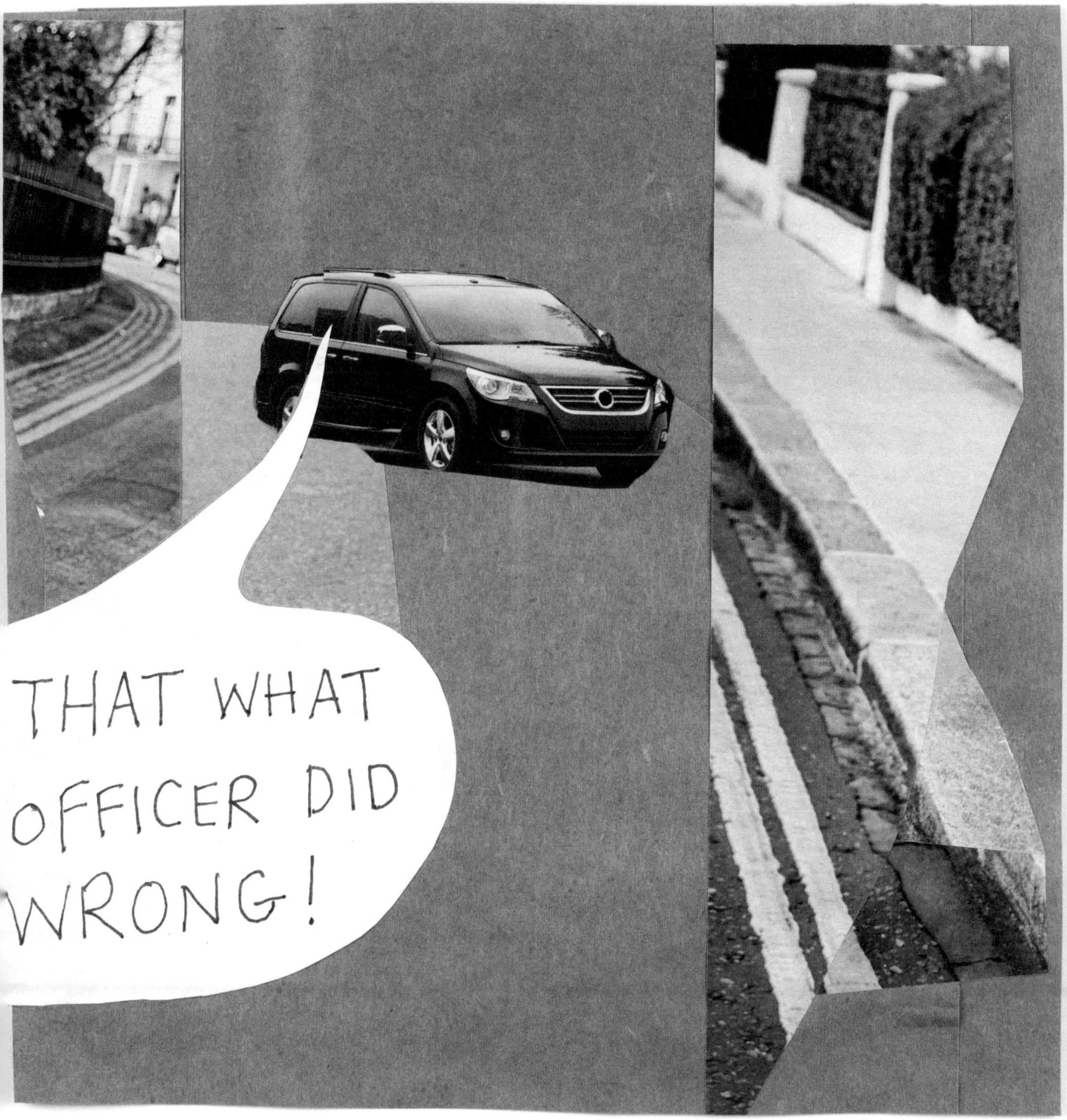
THAT WHAT OFFICER DID WRONG!

Go with your instincts on this one.
Racial justice is possible.

53

What do you
want it to say?

the end.

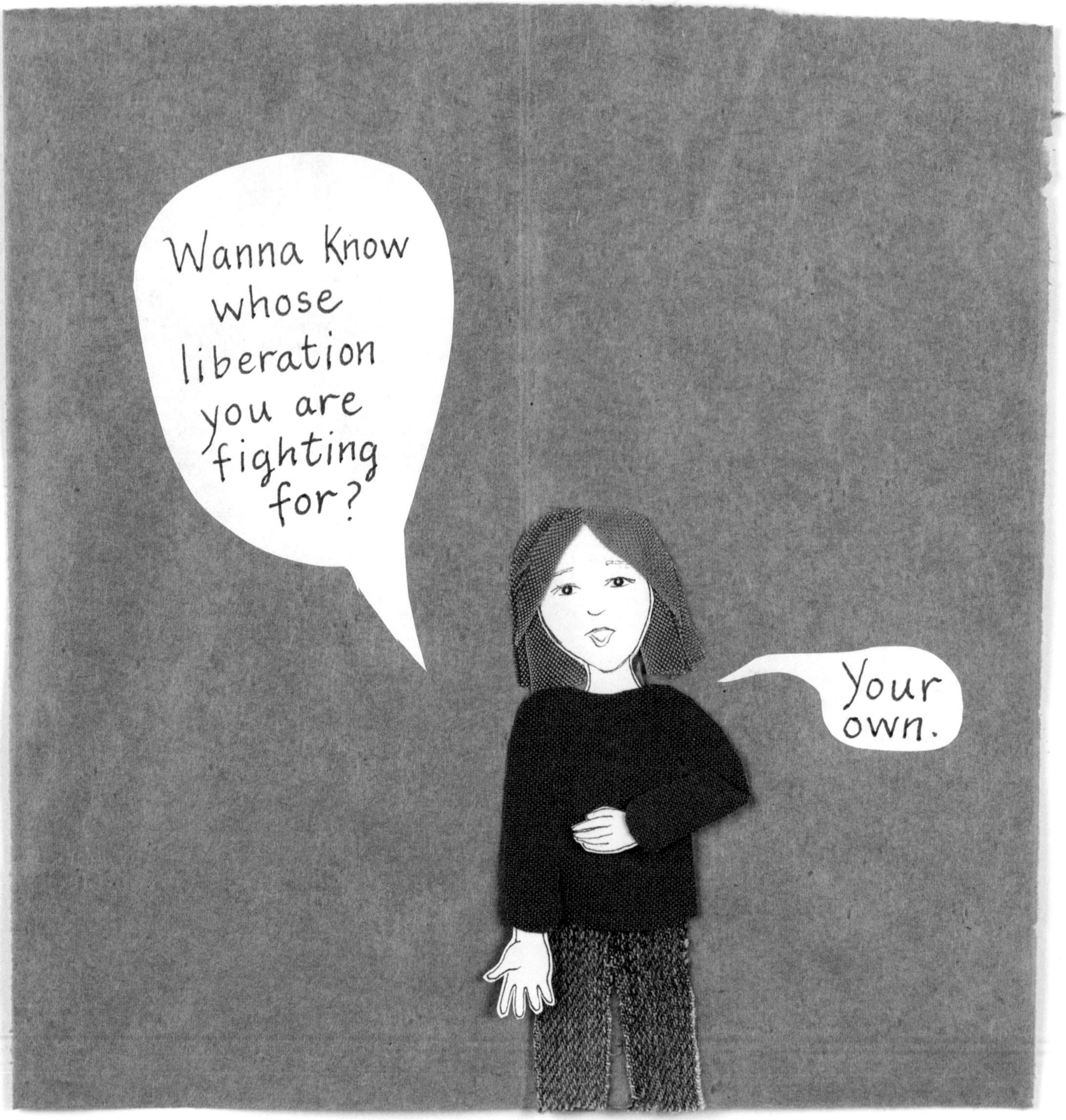
Wanna Know whose liberation you are fighting for?
Your own.

White supremacy has been lying to kids for centuries.

White supremacy is pretend. But the consequences are real.

The truth is much simpler.

dangerous

not dangerous

WHITENESS IS
A BAD DEAL.

It always was.

Dude, we can
see your
pointy tail.

Contract
Binding YOU to
WHITENESS
YOU get:
✓ stolen land
✓ stolen riches
✓ special favors †

WHITENESS gets:
✓ to mess endlessly
with the lives
of your friends,
neighbors, loved
ones, and all fellow
humans of
COLOR   for the
             purpose
             of
✓ your soul   profit
Sign below: $

_____

† Land, riches, and
favors may be revoked
at any time, for
any reason.

You can be WHITE without signing on to whiteness.

Juliette Hampton Morgan

Do not mess

with me.

Born 1914

Died 1957

...was a white librarian who fought for racial justice in Montgomery, Alabama. When Juliette was riding the bus and the white driver would refuse to pick up a Black bus rider — even after he collected their fare ($$$) — Juliette would pull the emergency cord and raise H-E-double-hockey-sticks until the driver did his job. This was an act of love, for herself and for the community to which she belonged. What she did is called: disrupting white supremacy.

A strong, internal sense of justice will not fail you—

even when a lack of justice in the world does.

Innocence
is
overrated.

Knowledge is Power

Color
this in ↗

Get some. Grow wise.
Make history.

Some people who *should be alive in this moment* are not. And *that* hurts.

Write their names here. Draw them a picture.

Show what's in you, even if you feel sad, or angry, or VERY SAD & VERY ANGRY
(this paper absorbs tears).

And if it's joy that you feel, let it flow.